MEET THE GIRL TALK CHARACTERS

Sabrina Wells is petite, with curly auburn hair, sparkling hazel eyes, and a bubbly personality. Sabrina loves magazines, shopping, sleepovers, and most of all, she loves talking to her best friends.

Katie Campbell is a straight-A student and super athlete. With her blond hair, blue eyes, and matching clothes, she's everyone's idea of Little Miss Perfect. But Katie has a few surprises for everyone, including herself!

Randy Zak has just moved to Acorn Falls from New York City, and is she ever cool! With her radical spiked haircut and her hip New York clothes, Randy teaches everyone just how much fun it is to be different.

Allison Cloud is a Native American Indian. Allison's supersmart and really beautiful. But she has one major problem: She's thirteen years old, five foot seven, and still growing!

IT'S ALL IN THE STARS

By L.E. Blair

GIRL TALK® series created by Western Publishing Company, Inc.

Western Publishing Company, Inc., Racine, Wisconsin 53404

Text by Carol McCarren

Chapter One

It looked like it was going to be one of those days. It was only eleven o'clock, and already I was going crazy. It was really warm outside, and we were supposed to be washing the car while Mom and Dad were out grocery shopping. But my brothers were washing *me* instead!

"Hey, Sabrina! Watch this!" my twin brother, Sam, shouted, pointing the hose and spraying me with water.

"Sam, cut it out! My hair's going to frizz," I pleaded, looking down at my soaking-wet jeans.

"'Sam, cut it out! My hair's going to frizz,'" he mimicked. Sam and I are both twelve, but Sam's always trying to boss me around because he's four whole minutes older than I am. Big deal!

"Bull's-eye!" cheered Mark, my third oldest

brother, as he showered the back of my shirt with water. Mark gave Sam a high five. Mark may be thirteen, but he sure doesn't act like it. He's always goofing around.

Having four older brothers definitely has its ups and downs, especially when they all gang up on me. When you're the youngest *and* the only girl, like I am, you do get a lot of attention and stuff. But there are so many of *them* that I can never win. For instance, if our parents give us a choice between going to a football game or going to a movie, we always end up going to the football game.

Anyway, I hate Saturday mornings because that's when everyone in my family does chores. The word *chores* makes it sound like we live on some big farm in Oklahoma instead of in a plain old house in Acorn Falls, Minnesota. Our house is pretty big, though, so it takes a lot of work to keep it clean. Dad says it's a Victorian house. It's painted white, with black shutters on all the windows, and there's a long porch in the front and a huge backyard.

I walked around to the back door and went inside, leaving a trail of puddles behind me. The inside of the house always seems just a little messy. Mom calls it the "lived-in" look. I was halfway across the kitchen before I remembered that she had just washed the floor. Great! Since I was dripping wet, I'd made it all muddy. I grabbed some paper towels and got down on my hands and knees to clean it up.

Just then, Luke, my second oldest brother, walked into the kitchen. As he opened the refrigerator for something to drink, he said, "That's right, Sabs. Stick to doing women's work!"

I could have killed him for that. He was just standing there, swigging down his soda like he was some famous rock star or something. He's been acting really cool since he turned sixteen and got his driver's license. Luke is a lot like Matthew, our oldest brother. Matt's eighteen and a freshman at college. He is my favorite brother, even though he was the one who started calling me "Blabs" instead of Sabs because I'm always on the phone with my friends.

I decided to ignore Luke. I finished wiping up the floor and went upstairs to my bedroom. I still had plenty of chores to do that morning, like clean the living room and dining room, clear the dishwasher, and clean my room. Since I was already in my room, I decided to get that part over with first.

My room is in the attic, and it's really big. I have to admit that by Saturday it's usually pretty messy. Luckily my mom did the laundry, so I put clean sheets on my bed, put away my clean clothes and put all my magazines in neat stacks. When I finished, I sat down on a chair and looked around. My room looked beautiful. Then I started thinking about the sleepover I was having that night with my friends Katie Campbell, Randy Zak, and Allison Cloud. I still had a million things to do before they arrived. Suddenly I remembered that I hadn't read my horoscope yet. I can't do anything until I read my horoscope. I wondered how I had made it through the morning without it.

I ran down to the kitchen, grabbed the newspaper, and turned to page twelve. The horoscope section is always on page twelve. I read it once, then double-checked to make sure the prediction was for the right sign. It said: *Pisces: Be ready for love and new contacts. It is wise to get in touch with your spiritual side. Romance is coming. Keep following the stars.*

4

I put the paper down and ran over to the dishwasher to put away the clean dishes. Wow! A romance prediction! I wondered what *Be ready for love* meant. But I couldn't believe that it said to *get in touch with your spiritual side*, because that was exactly what I had been doing! I'd taken this great book out of the library, *Madame Pandora's Guide to a Better Planet*. I also planned on having a séance at my sleepover. I couldn't believe that my horoscope was so totally right.

A look at my hot-pink watch told me that I was running out of time. I still had a million things to do. Everyone was supposed to be at my house by five o'clock. And it was already two-thirty!

I must have vacuumed and dusted the whole house in about six minutes flat. Then I raced down to the basement. That's where I had decided to hold the séance. I grabbed an old flowered purple curtain and threw it over the card table.

Next I had to find a crystal ball. The closest thing we had was Luke's fishbowl, but the fish were still in it. I didn't want to make a big deal out of the whole thing. I knew that Luke would ask me a bunch of questions about why I wanted to borrow his fishbowl. So I just ran upstairs, grabbed it off the end table in the living room, lugged it to the basement, and plopped it down in the middle of the table. The bowl didn't exactly look magical with the fish swimming in it, but in the dark nobody would really be able to tell the difference.

I pulled four chairs up to the table and stood back to look at the effect. Not bad, but it was definitely too bright down here for a séance. Séances in the movies are always dark and spooky, and I wanted to make this as close to the real thing as I could. Then it hit me — candles! A couple of flickering candles would add just the right touch. I went upstairs to look for some just as my parents walked into the kitchen with bags of groceries.

"Mom, I'm putting on sort of a show tonight at my sleepover, and I need a couple of candles," I said, trying to look as innocent as I could.

"No way!" my mother said firmly. "No more candles in this house — ever! Have you forgotten how you and Sam almost burned the house down last Halloween?" she asked, raising her eyebrows at me.

How could I forget? Mom brings it up every time anyone mentions the word *candles*. Okay, so we made a little mistake. Last Halloween, Sam and I and Nick Robbins, one of Sam's best friends, carved out this great pumpkin. It looked really good, but Sam decided that it needed a hat. So we put a candle in the pumpkin and stuck one of my dad's wool ski hats on top. The thing is, we forgot to put the top of the pumpkin back on first. The pumpkin sat in the window for almost an hour. Then the hat caught on fire and the smoke alarm in the kitchen went off. Mom and Dad got pretty mad about the whole thing. I admit, the house did smell kind of funny for a while, but I thought it was pretty harsh treatment for Sam and me to be grounded for a month. On top of that we had to buy a new hat for my dad.

I could tell there was no way Mom was going to give in about the candles. This was definitely a major problem. Candles are so important for atmosphere, and atmosphere is what séances are all about.

I decided to forget the candles for a while

and work on my outfit for the séance. Clothes are also very important in things like this. If I was going to lead this séance, I would have to look the part. I chose a long red plaid flannel nightgown. My white blanket made a shawl. Not exactly mystical-looking, but it would have to do. I added a pair of big hoop earrings and a bunch of necklaces that my Aunt Pat had given me for Christmas. The necklaces were all tangled, but they looked good that way.

Next I experimented with my hair. First I tied a big gold-and-black print scarf around my head. But, with my red hair, the earrings and the scarf made me look like a circus clown. I decided that Madame Pandora would never hold a séance looking like this. Maybe a turban would do the trick. I tried a big orange towel, wrapping it the way I do after I wash my hair. But my hair is so thick when it's dry that the towel kept popping off. What was I going to do? I looked at my watch again. I didn't have much time.

I quickly rummaged through my closet, and the answer literally fell on my head — my bathing cap! I tucked my hair under the yellow cap and wrapped the towel into a turban over it. I used a couple of hairpins to hold the towel in place. Then I clipped a big green dangling earring to the turban so the earring would hang right in the middle of my forehead. Perfect! "Madame Sabrina," I said, laughing to myself, "you look marvelous!"

I stuffed everything but the nightgown into a bag and ran down to the basement to put it someplace safe. That way, when the time came, I could change in the basement and not have to walk through the house looking like a weirdo. If any of my brothers figured out what I was trying to do, they'd ruin the whole thing.

But I still hadn't figured out the candle problem. *Be creative*, I thought. I'm a Pisces with Sagittarius rising. I'm supposed to be good at this kind of stuff. The phrase *keep following the stars* kept running through my mind. Suddenly I had a brilliant idea.

I went into my dad's workshop and took one of his screwdrivers. I used the screwdriver to punch holes into a couple of coffee cans I found lying around. Then I took two flashlights from the family's camping gear, which we keep on shelves in the basement. I stood the flashlights up, turned them on, and covered them with the cans. Then I turned out all the lights in the basement. The whole place was full of stars. It looked great! I shut off the flashlights and ran back upstairs and got into the shower. After all the running around I'd been doing, I really needed it.

I had just turned off the blow dryer when I heard the doorbell ring. I checked my watch. Five o'clock exactly. What timing! I ran downstairs to answer the door.

Chapter Two

"Hi, Katie," I said as I opened the door. Katie was fumbling with her luggage, but even when Katie fumbles, she looks neat and organized. She was wearing a soft pink sweater and blue jeans with a pink belt. Her jeans were rolled up a little and I noticed that she was even wearing pink socks. She had her hair tied back with a pink ribbon. She always color-coordinates her accessories, just like the magazine articles say you should.

Katie's a little taller than I am, and she has straight honey-blond hair and blue eyes. She looks great in all the styles you see in *Young Chic*, my favorite magazine. I try to keep up with the latest fashions, but for some reason clothes don't look quite the same on me as they do in the magazines. Maybe it's because I'm only four foot ten and three-quarter inches.

"Is anyone else here yet?" she asked when

she finished fumbling.

Just then the doorbell rang. It was Randy. Her real name is Rowena Zak, but she won't let anyone call her that. Randy's from New York City. She has spiked black hair and dark eyes. When she gets angry, her eyes actually turn black. It's kind of cool.

Randy has a great sense of style, too. Tonight she was wearing one of her SoHo outfits. She had on a black miniskirt, a black turtleneck sweater, purple-and-green leggings, a bunch of beaded bracelets, and wild earrings. And, of course, she was wearing her black leather jacket. I've always wanted a leather jacket, but my mom says it's really silly to buy such an expensive jacket while I'm still growing.

"Take these," she commanded, handing me a stack of cassette tapes. "My mom's waiting in the car. I've got to go back and get the rest of my stuff."

"I'll help," Katie offered, dumping her bags in the hallway.

Within minutes, the hallway was filled with junk. Just as Randy's mom was pulling out of the driveway, a dark green Volvo pulled up across the street. We watched as Allison Cloud kissed her father good-bye, got out of the car, and ran across the street. Allison is very graceful, and very tall. She's at least five foot seven.

Sometimes I wish I looked like Allison. Allison is Chippewa, a Native American. She has waist-length black hair that she always wears in a braid. She has big brown eyes, and she's just — well, I don't know quite how to explain it. She's shy and quiet, and her voice is really soft. My mom always says that Allison is very ladylike. She calls her "an exotic beauty." I wish someone would describe me that way.

Al was wearing red corduroy pants with a red-checked blouse that had a Peter Pan collar, and she looked just great! I'd look like a Christmas elf in an outfit like that. I have to admit that sometimes I get a little jealous of the way my friends look.

"Can you believe it?" Randy said, reading my mind. "Al's only got one bag!" We eyed the huge pile of pillows, sleeping bags, and cassette tapes that Randy and Katie had dumped in the hallway and laughed.

"What's so funny?" Allison asked, coming through the door.

"Is that all you brought?" Randy teased Allison. "One bag?"

"What else do I need?" Allison asked. "It's just for one night."

Allison is always so logical.

"Well, let's get this show on the road," I announced loudly. "Everybody grab your stuff and bring it up to my room." We rushed up to my room and set up the sleeping bags. The one good thing about being the only girl in the family is that I get the entire attic to myself.

Randy couldn't wait to play her newest rock tape for us. Randy really loves music. She's pretty talented, too. She can play the drums, and she's trying to teach herself to play the guitar. When she lived in New York, she took all kinds of music lessons. She's always talking about the cool concerts her dad took her to see at Madison Square Garden, and about visiting him on location when he was directing music videos. But that was before her parents got divorced and she moved to Acorn Falls.

Then my dad called us downstairs for dinner. He had gone out and gotten a couple of pizzas and some soda. The way we ran downstairs, you'd think we hadn't eaten for a week. While we were eating, I tried to figure out how to get everybody in the mood for a séance. I just wasn't sure they would go for it. Katie, Randy, and Al don't pay as much attention to horoscopes as I do. In fact, Randy makes fun of them.

Suddenly I got a great idea. The last time we had a sleepover at Katie's, we really got into playing levitation. It's this cool game where you try to lift somebody off the floor by using only the power of your mind. At one point, we almost had Katie in the air, but then Katie's sister, Emily, came in and broke the spell.

"Hey, let's play levitation," I suggested.

"Oh, no, not that again," Randy moaned.

"It almost worked last time," Katie reminded her.

"Yeah. Let's try it again!" I urged, looking straight at Allison.

"I'll do it," she agreed.

"Maybe we need more people," Katie suggested.

"Probably," I agreed. "But, I'm not about to ask any of my brothers."

"So what should we do?" Randy said, sounding a little bored.

"Let's go down to the basement."

"The basement?" Katie asked, looking at me as if I had two heads. "What for?"

"Well, it's kind of stuffy up here." I was trying not to give anything away. "And besides, I've planned something really cool."

"Like what?" Katie asked.

"A séance," I blurted out. I hadn't meant to tell them yet, but it just popped out. I held my breath, waiting to hear what they would say.

"A séance! Wow, that sounds like fun," Katie squealed.

"It might not be so bad," Allison said, considering carefully.

I couldn't believe it. They were really into it! I was just starting to feel relieved when Randy ruined the whole thing.

"Oh, no, Sabrina," she said. "You're not going to start all that hocus-pocus junk again, are you?"

"Oh, come on, Randy. It'll be fun," Katie said. "Don't be a party pooper."

"We could contact John Lennon," Allison added quietly. Wow! Why hadn't I thought of that? Randy loves John Lennon. Her eyes lit up at the mention of his name. I could have kissed Al for thinking of it.

"Yeah," I put in quickly. "We could ask him all kinds of questions about what it was like to be a member of the Beatles."

"John Lennon?" Randy repeated. She looked interested in spite of herself.

"We could try," said Katie eagerly, giving me a secret wink.

"Well, I don't really believe in this stuff," Randy said finally, "but if you guys reach John Lennon you're going to need somebody down there who knows something about music."

I made them all wait for me at the top of the basement stairs while I put on my costume and turned on the flashlight stars. Then I called them down, turned off the regular light, and waited for their reactions.

The only light in the basement was coming from the flashlight stars, and the shadows they made were actually creepy. Even Luke's gold-fish were acting weird, swimming back and forth really fast. The light made the purple flowers on the tablecloth look almost like strange, magic symbols.

"Awesome, Sabrina," Randy said.

"Wow! We should do this for Halloween. It's so spooky down here," Katie exclaimed.

"It is," Allison agreed.

"Well, let's not make a big deal out of it. It's just a game," Randy reminded us. I was kind of glad to hear that, because I didn't have the slightest idea of how to get in touch with John Lennon from my basement. "Cool outfit, Sabs. Can I borrow those earrings sometime?" Randy asked.

"You look like a gypsy or something," Allison put in, smiling.

"Yeah," said Katie, grinning, "and there's even something to see in your crystal ball!"

"Seet down, seet down, my cheeldren," I began, using my Madame Pandora voice. I don't know why, but I just love imitating weird accents. Randy sat across from me, Allison sat to my left, and Katie was on my right. "Let us all join hands," I instructed.

"Um, Sabrina, I think you're supposed to just touch fingers," Allison interrupted. "Like this." She laid her hands flat on the table to demonstrate. "I mean, that's what I've read."

"Oh, yeah," I replied. "I wasn't sure." I

cleared my throat. "And now I vill chant in order to get een touch vith the speerits on the other side," I continued. "Oommmm," I chanted with my eyes shut. "Oommmm." Katie started to giggle.

"What are you laughing at?" I asked her.

"I think you have to mention John Lennon's name," Katie said, still giggling.

I felt kind of dumb sitting there with an orange towel wrapped around my head and being the only one chanting. "Okay. So you guys start chanting with me and we'll say John Lennon's name between chants," I ordered, shifting nervously in my chair.

"Okay. Everyone close your eyes and touch fingers," I continued. I began to chant, "Oommmm. John Lennon. Oommmm. John Lennon. John Len-non. Jo-ohn Len-non!" We all started to giggle uncontrollably.

"Cut it out, Sabrina," Randy begged. "My stomach is killing me!"

I lifted my hands over my crystal ball and spoke. "Ees anyone there? Oh, great speerits on the other side, vee are trying to contact John Lennon."

We were trying our best to be serious, but

we couldn't stop laughing. And even though everyone was supposed to have their eyes closed, I could see that we were all peeking.

"John, eef you can hear us, show us a sign," I went on. We waited. No answer. "Oommmm. John. Oommmm. Lennon," I began again. I knew I was probably making funny faces, but I couldn't help it.

"Sabrina! Stop! You're making me die," Randy pleaded again.

"John, eef you can hear us, knock three times," I went on. By this time we were laughing really hard. Then, all of a sudden, we heard a loud knock. It sounded really strange, kind of hollow. Then we heard a second knock. It was definitely coming from somewhere near the ceiling. We all got really quiet. Then there was a third knock.

All of a sudden we were all holding hands instead of touching fingers. Katie gripped my hand so tightly that I couldn't feel my fingers. We waited for what seemed like hours, but nothing else happened. Finally I couldn't stand it any longer. I cleared my throat.

"Who-who d-did that?" I asked shakily.

"This-is-John-Lennon," a deep voice

boomed suddenly. "Who stole my guitar?"

"Yikes!" I screamed. Allison dived under the table, yelling something. Katie eased up the death grip on my hand and jumped out of her seat. With a loud crash, everything fell to the floor — table, flashlight "stars," tablecloth, and goldfish bowl.

After the crash, the whole basement went quiet again. Now it was pitch-black, and we were even more nervous than before. I kept waiting for something to happen, but nothing did. I was just about to open my mouth when I heard Sam's all-too-familiar voice.

"I'm sorry, Sabrina. What happened?"

"Sam Wells! Where are you? I'm going to kill you!" I stumbled around in the dark until I found him near the stairs. I grabbed him by the neck and wrestled him to the floor.

Suddenly the lights were switched on, and mom and dad were standing at the top of the steps, staring at the mess. "What in the world is going on down here?" my mother asked.

Blinking from the bright lights, I looked around the basement. The card table and chairs were all overturned. There were two flashlights, two cans with holes, and a fishbowl with a huge crack in it on top of the flow-ered curtain. The water from the fishbowl was all over the floor, and the fish were....

"Oh, no!" I yelped, scrambling to my feet. "Come on, everybody, help me find the fish. Please! Luke's going to kill me! Hurry! They might still be alive!"

We all got down on our knees and started to hunt for the fish. "Now I'm really dead," I kept repeating. "Luke's going to slaughter me if I killed his fish."

Sam ran up to the kitchen to get bottled water. Then he poured some in a plastic bowl for the fish. We all scooped up the fish and dropped them into the bowl. Eventually we saved them all.

"We'll talk about this tomorrow," my moth-er said when we were done.

"But I want the basement cleaned tonight," my father added. The two of them left, shaking their heads in disbelief. During the entire time we were straightening up, I kept hearing little giggling sounds from Allison, Katie, and Randy. I just tried to ignore them. When we were finished, I glared at Sam. "Thanks for get-ting me into trouble, Sam."

"I didn't mean it, Sabrina. It was just a joke!" Sam began. "I was hiding in the closet, listening. When you said to knock three times, I just picked up a broom and banged on the hot water pipes, and..." Then, he turned around completely, pointed to my head, and let out the wildest laugh I've ever heard. "What are you doing with a bathing cap on your head?" My friends had their hands over their mouths, trying to stifle their own laughter.

My hands flew to my head as I realized that my turban had fallen off in all the excitement. With my big hoop earrings, I must have looked like something out of *Star Trek*. I gasped and ripped the cap off my head.

"Now your hair's all stuck to your head. You look like a moldy onion!" Sam gasped. He laughed so hard that tears came to his eyes.

"It's not funny!" I told him angrily. That just made all of them laugh harder. I looked at Sam and my best friends, who by now were rolling around on the floor, laughing. I felt giggles welling up inside me, too, but there was no way I was going to let Sam see me laughing. I started up the stairs to my room, motion-

23

ing for my friends to follow. When we got to my room, we were all still laughing.

"Okay," I said after we had calmed down. "Maybe it was just a little bit funny."

"A little bit?" Randy asked, wiping tears from her eyes. "You looked so funny yelling at Sam with that bathing cap…"

"…and those earrings!" Katie added, hugging a pillow and falling back on the bed with laughter.

"Traitors," I joked, throwing a pillow at Katie. Then Katie tossed the pillow to Al. Al threw one at Randy, who threw one at me, and we ended up having this big pillow fight.

"Anyone for ice cream?" asked Mark, poking his head into the room. "Mom says we can make sundaes if you guys promise not to destroy the kitchen."

Well, sundaes certainly weren't part of my self-improvement program, but after the night I'd had, I certainly deserved one. We all marched down to the kitchen and happily pigged out on hot fudge and ice cream.

Chapter Three

On Monday morning the whole family was in the kitchen eating breakfast. Our kitchen is bright and cheerful, decorated in yellow and white, with lots of sun because of all the windows.

"Would someone please ask Sam to pass me the C Section of the newspaper?" I said in my most formal voice. I was definitely not going to talk to him myself. I was still totally mad at him for ruining my séance and getting me in trouble.

My mother sighed. "Your brother has apologized enough," she said. "Now start acting like a human being and talk to him."

"Why do I always get yelled at when he does something wrong?" I protested.

"You destroyed my goldfish bowl," Luke reminded me. I could tell he wasn't *that* mad about it. I was just in trouble because I hadn't asked if I could borrow it first. Now Sam and I had to save our allowances and split the cost of buying a new one. I never have any money left over at the end of the week. It was going to take me forever to earn that much. Thank goodness we'd saved all the fish.

"Sam, give your sister Section C," my father said, finishing his coffee. Sam handed it over. First I made believe that I was interested in an article on the front page. Then I casually turned to the horoscope section. The page was ripped out! Fuming, I glanced in Sam's direction.

"Looking for this?" He smiled, waving the page.

"Give it to me, Sam!" I yelled at him. I stood up and walked around the table toward him.

Dramatically, he held the page like a scroll, extended his pinkies, and read aloud, "*It's a good day for phone calls, letters, and love. Someone tall, dark, and gorgeous adores you. Watch for secret declarations. Aquarius plays an important role.* I'm tall, redheaded, and gorgeous," Sam joked. He reached for my hand and kissed it.

To be honest, I wasn't really listening. I was

beginning to get excited. Another love prediction. It made my heart pound, and I got a funny feeling in my stomach. I made sure I kept a straight face, though. If I let my brothers see how much this prediction meant to me, they would never stop teasing me about it.

"I'll be late for school," I announced, grabbing my books and running out the door. All the way to school I kept thinking about my tall, dark, and gorgeous admirer and wondering who it could be. So it was definitely a shock when I walked into math class and saw Miss Munson putting papers face down on each desk.

"Oh, no!" I gasped. I had forgotten all about my math test!

"Is something the matter, Miss Wells?" Miss Munson asked, scowling. Teachers like Miss Munson, who've been teaching for a billion years, develop a way of knowing when students aren't ready for class. Miss Munson only pays attention to me when I don't know the answer or haven't studied. She also happens to be known as the Dragon Lady. She's a real grouch a lot of the time.

"No, everything's fine, Miss Munson," I

answered, shooting a desperate glance at Katie. But she was reading through her notes and didn't even see me. I sat down at my desk and pulled out a pencil with a really big eraser. I had the feeling that I was going to need it.

The test was all word problems, and I kept getting more and more confused. Word problems are always so weird. I mean, who cares how much money Jack has if he has twenty-eight percent of what Mary has plus thirty-seven percent of what Peter has? I just wished I had some of whatever Jack had so I could pay for Luke's stupid fishbowl. By the end of first period both my eraser and my good mood were gone. It wasn't until lunch that I started to feel a little better.

"Wow, this morning really went fast," Randy said as we sat down in the cafeteria. Randy, Katie, Al, and I eat lunch together every single day. "But I can't wait for the end of the day."

"Does anyone want to come over to my house after school?" Allison asked. "I have to baby-sit for Charlie." Charlie is Allison's seven-year-old brother. He's really cute.

"Sure," said Katie and Randy together.

"Okay. I'll meet you over there," I said. "I have to return some books to the school library." It was time to get rid of Madame Pandora once and for all.

At the end of the day, I dropped off my library books and then went back to my locker to get my dirty gym clothes. Katie and I share a locker, and I think the fact that I'm a little messy sometimes bothers her. Katie's a Virgo, and Virgos can be very, very picky. But I can understand how she feels. I have this terrible habit of leaving my gym clothes in there a little too long.

As usual, one of my socks was missing. No matter what I do, I always manage to lose one sock. I stood on my tiptoes to search the top shelf. But instead of finding my missing sock, I found an envelope. It was pink, with flowers all over it. At first I thought it was Katie's, but it had my name written on the front. I had no idea what it was because I didn't recognize the handwriting. I opened it and unfolded the cutest little note on pink stationery. It had a little red heart sticker on it. My heart leaped at the first line:

My Dear Sabrina,
    I can't stop thinking about you. You are like a beautiful flower. I can see your face in all my dreams. I know that someday we will be together. Till then, my love, here is my heart.

Your Secret Admirer

I immediately felt my famous body blush beginning. When that happens I feel like I'm about to burn up and my whole body gets red and blotchy. I sure hoped my secret admirer wasn't around to see. It was just like my horoscope had predicted — *a good day for phone calls, letters, and love.*

My heart was beating a million miles an hour. Forgetting all about my gym clothes and my missing sock, I practically flew over to Allison's house. When I burst into the house, Randy and Katie were sitting at the dining-room table with Allison and Charlie, studying and eating chocolate-chunk cookies.

"You're never going to believe this," I said, sitting down to catch my breath. I held out the note as I dropped my knapsack to the floor. Randy took it from my hand.

As Randy read the note out loud, her eyes

widened. Allison leaned over the table to hear better. All at once Katie gasped, and grabbed the note from Randy's hand.

"*Till then, my love, here is my heart,*" Katie read, getting really excited. "*Your Secret Admirer.* Wow! A secret admirer!"

"Who do you think it is?" Allison asked.

"I have no idea," I answered. "But this is exactly what my horoscope said would happen."

"Oh, come off it, Sabrina. Horoscope — horrorscope!" Randy said, laughing. "Those things are never right!"

"Never right, huh? I'll show you, word for word," I replied, grabbing a cookie. "Allison, do you have today's newspaper around?"

"Yes, it's probably in the living room," she said. "I'll go get it."

While we waited, I looked around. Allison's house is really old like mine, but her parents have restored it. The floors are all wood and the walls have dark wooden paneling, so you'd think the inside would be really dark. But Mrs. Cloud had hung up all these straw baskets and light-colored wall hangings to brighten it up. And there are bright, green, airy plants all over the place, and lots of windows for natural lighting. It's always super clean and kind of, well, formal compared to my house. But it's really cool at the same time.

"Here it is," Al said, handing me the paper. I turned to the horoscope section and Randy read it out loud. *"It's a good day for phone calls, letters, and love. Someone tall, dark, and gorgeous adores you. Watch for secret declarations. Aquarius plays an important role."* Then she looked up at me, frowning.

"It's just a coincidence, Sabs," Randy said. "These horoscopes are totally phony. Even Charlie wouldn't believe them."

"But, Randy," Katie said, "Sabrina's horoscope mentions a secret letter from a tall, dark, and gorgeous admirer."

"Anybody want a soda?" Allison asked, leading us into the kitchen. Even the kitchen at her house has lots of wood in it. The floor is regular kitchen tile, but there's a big wooden island in the middle with six wooden stools, and all the cupboards and storage boxes are varnished wood.

"Got any diet soda?" I asked. I always try to cut calories whenever I can. It's part of my self-improvement plan, especially after a weekend of pizza and ice-cream sundaes.

"Are you sure your horoscope says it's okay to drink soda today?" Randy teased. "Or do you have to wait for a lunar eclipse?"

"Oh, stop it, Randy," Katie said. "This time Sabs is right."

"It was pretty accurate," Allison agreed. "But who could your secret admirer be? Tall and dark-haired..." Her forehead wrinkled as she thought about it.

"I don't think I know anybody like that," I said.

"Wait a minute!" Katie exclaimed. "What about Jason McKee?"

"Jason?" I said, surprised. I couldn't help thinking that Jason McKee was cute, but he sure wasn't my idea of tall, dark, and gorgeous.

"Well, that's a sign," Katie told me. "I mean, we all know that Sam has a crush on Stacy Hansen now, right?"

"Right," I agreed, making a face. Stacy Hansen is the most popular girl in our school and she knows it. Katie, Al, Randy, and I don't like her very much, and she doesn't like us either. But just last week I found a piece of paper in our living room with "Sam + Stacy" written on it. I brought it up to Sam's room and gave it to him, just to see what he would do. He turned bright red, grabbed the paper, and slammed his door in my face. When I told the girls the next day, we all decided to watch him. We noticed that whenever Stacy was around, Sam would keep looking at her and blushing. He definitely had a major crush on Stacy Hansen, and we all knew it.

"Well," Katie continued, "I heard him tell Nick and Jason that he thinks Stacy's a real pain. And he never talks to her or anything. If Sam told his friends that he liked Stacy, they would never stop teasing him. Maybe Jason just doesn't want anyone to know that he likes you because he's afraid of being teased, too."

"Tall and dark-haired," Allison repeated for the second time.

"It's Jason," Randy decided. "He's tall, and he's dark, and he's always hanging around Sabrina's house. Yeah, it's got to be Jason McKee."

"I think so too," Katie agreed. "I always had a feeling he could be very romantic."

We all decided right then and there that Jason McKee was definitely the one, but secretly I wasn't so sure. I've always had the feeling that I was destined for great things — greater than Jason McKee, anyway.

To me, Jason McKee is tall, dark, and *cute*. But my secret admirer was supposed to be tall, dark, and *gorgeous*. There's a big difference between a cute guy and gorgeous one. I concentrated on thinking about the guys at school who I thought were gorgeous.

Well, there's Eric Bryner, I thought to myself. He's an eighth grader and the captain of the wrestling team. Eric knows my brother Mark, but he's never been to our house. I was pretty sure he had a girlfriend, though. I would have to check.

And there was Alec. I'd had a crush on him at the beginning of the year, but I didn't anymore. And Randy's friend Spike, but we were definitely just friends. Anyway, I hardly ever see him, since he's in high school.

Maybe it was Brian Stephens! He was so cute he could win a Patrick Swayze look-alike contest. He plays the saxophone in the school band, but I've never even talked to him. I only know his name because I heard the band teacher, Mr. Metcalf, call on him. He smiled at me once, though.

Anyone else? I racked my brains, but the only other person I could come up with was my social studies teacher, Damien Grey. Mr. Grey is the most gorgeous teacher I've ever had — he looks like an older and more sophisticated version of Tom Cruise! But it would be ridiculous to think that he could be my secret admirer. I mean, he's so much older than I am.

"I can't believe how seriously you're taking this," Randy said, staring at me.

"I guess it's not every day you get a letter from a secret admirer," Allison reminded her.

"That's right, " I mumbled. But inside I was wondering how we could discover who my secret admirer really was. I just knew it wasn't Jason. It was definitely someone totally special and amazing. He would probably turn out to be the love of my life and sweep me off my feet. I mean, this secret admirer could change my destiny forever. The whole idea gave me goose bumps.

Chapter Four

The next day I got up an hour earlier than usual so I could get to school early. I really wanted to find out who my secret admirer was. Maybe I could catch him slipping another note into my locker. I had stayed up late to practice my clarinet and to reread the two chapters we were supposed to know for social studies. I wanted to impress my admirer, whether it was Brian Stephens from band or my social studies teacher, Mr. Grey. I was pretty sure it wasn't Eric Bryner, because my brother Matt told me that Eric already had a girlfriend.

I also had to get up early if I wanted to use the bathroom for more than two minutes. With all those brothers around, it was almost impossible to get a minute to myself in there. After my shower, I rushed back to my room to pick out my clothes. I decided on my blue denim skirt, a white cotton turtleneck, and my red plaid blazer. I had always hated the blazer but suddenly it seemed just right. My grandmother had given it to me for my birthday, and I thought it was really uncool. I only wore it when my mother insisted, like when we went to a family dinner or something like that. But suddenly I realized that the blazer made me look a little older and kind of sophisticated. That was exactly what I wanted.

Then I realized that I didn't have any shoes that would go with my outfit. I had a pair of red flats, but if I was supposed to look more mature, I definitely had to be taller than four foot ten and three-quarter inches. I finally ended up wearing a pair of low-heeled white pumps that my mother had given me. I had bugged her for heels so much that she gave them to me to practice in until I was ready to get a pair of my own. They were about an inch too long and a little too wide, but I stuffed some tissues in the toes and they worked just fine.

When I finished dressing, I started on my hair. I wanted to make sure that my hair looked just right. I had seen this really great hairstyle in *Young Chic* that was supposed to make you look mature, and I wanted to try it out. The style was kind of a French twist. It took forever to get my hair pinned up the way the picture showed. Since my hair is so curly, I had to use a lot of mousse to keep it from frizzing, but the result looked really good.

Finally I went down to the kitchen. No one had come down yet so I decided to read my horoscope while I ate breakfast. *Confusion surrounds your social life. Guard your secrets carefully. You have your own private dreams to dream. A family member tries to make peace.* Well, there was nothing about romance this time, but I sure was confused about my social life. I had to figure out who my secret admirer was!

When I got to school, I put the blazer in my locker until it was time for social studies. I didn't want it to get all wrinkled. Besides, I just knew that Randy, Katie, and Allison would ask me all kinds of questions about it. They had sure heard me complain about the blazer the last time my mom had made me wear it.

We got our tests back in math class. Considering the fact that I hadn't studied, I was pretty happy with my B-minus.

After math, I ran straight to my locker to get my clarinet for band. Then I rushed to the practice room to see if Brian Stephens was there. I walked into the room and there he was! He was walking to the storage closet at the back of the room to get a music stand. He pushed his dark hair back from his forehead and said something to one of the guys in the drum section.

I quickly put my clarinet on my seat, checked to make sure that my hair was still in place, and went to get a stand for myself. When Brian turned around, I was standing right behind him. He looked so much like Patrick Swayze that I could hardly believe it. I just stood there, staring at him. My heart was beating so loudly that I was afraid he would hear it, even over the sounds of all the people in the band room.

"Uh, hi," he muttered.

"Hi, Brian," I breathed. "I just came over to get a music stand."

"Yeah," he said, giving me a strange look. Then I realized how stupid I must have sounded. There's nothing in the storage closet *but* music stands. I felt my body blush beginning.

Brian started to walk away.

"Great job, bingo brain!" I muttered to myself. I always make such a fool out of myself! I grabbed a stand and started back to my seat.

"Hey, wait a second," said a voice. It was Brian! "Aren't you Sam Wells's sister? Sarah, or something like that?" he asked.

"Sabrina," I corrected him, totally embarrassed. He didn't even know my name! How could I ever have thought that he was my secret admirer?

"Yeah, Sabrina. Well, would you ask Sam to give me a call? I need someone to shoot some hoops with me before tryouts."

"I'll tell him," I mumbled as I walked away. I couldn't believe I'd actually thought that Brian Stephens liked me! I sat down and waited for Mr. Metcalf to start practice. Why was I always jumping to conclusions? I usually love band practice but suddenly my heart wasn't in it, and Mr. Metcalf kept giving me strange looks.

I was pretty depressed until lunchtime. I filled my tray and went to sit with Katie, Randy, and Allison. As soon as I sat down

Randy asked Katie about the social studies assignment, and it suddenly hit me. If Eric Bryner had a girlfriend, and Brian Stephens didn't even know who I was, that meant there was a good chance that Mr. Grey was my tall, dark, and gorgeous admirer! I thought about it for a while and realized that I should have known it from the beginning. No seventh- or eighth-grade boy could have written that note. It was much too mature and romantic. Besides, who else could it be?

I was in a daze for the rest of the day. Instead of taking notes in class, I wrote his name over and over in my notebook — *Damien Grey*. I wished that I knew when his birthday was. I just had to find out if he was an Aquarius or not. If he was, then he was definitely my secret admirer.

The more I thought about it, the more sure I got. On the last homework assignment he had returned to me, Mr. Grey had written, "Great job, Sabs!" and had drawn a smiley face. None of my teachers had ever used my nickname before. And why would he take all the extra time to write me a note and draw that smiley face if he didn't think I was special? There was one last thing that absolutely proved it. I had found the note in my locker, right? Well, only two people knew the combination for that locker — Katie and I. And neither of us would tell anyone, so how could it have been another student? But Mr. Grey is a teacher. If he wanted to find out a locker combination, all he had to do was ask at the office! I couldn't wait for seventh period. I'd never been so excited about going to class before in my entire life.

After sixth period I stopped by my locker to pick up the blazer. Then I ran to the bathroom to check my hair. I had to rush because I wanted to get to class early. I usually sit with Randy and Katie. But I wanted to sit in the first seat in the first row. That way Mr. Grey would be sure to notice me. And I figured that sitting alone without my friends would make me look more like an independent woman.

I was just putting on my blazer and getting settled when Winslow Barton, the class nerd, took the seat right next to mine. I almost died when I saw what he was wearing. Winslow always wears a blazer. And today he had on a red plaid one that looked exactly like mine. Now I remembered why I'd hated my blazer so much when I got it. It reminded me of Winslow! Well, there was nothing I could do about it. I just had to sit there looking like Winslow Barton's clone. How was I supposed to impress Mr. Grey now?

See, Winslow is probably the guy they used as a model when they made those movies about nerds. He has a buzz crew cut, which makes him look like he's in the marines or something. He wears heavy black-framed glasses, pants that are too short, white socks, and dress shoes. He actually has plastic pocket protectors in the pockets of all his blazers, and he carries about a million pens all the time. Randy's gotten to know him pretty well because they both like computer music a lot, and she says he's really not a nerd. Randy thinks it's cool that he's so different, but I still think he's kind of weird.

Randy's voice jolted me out of my thoughts and I looked up just as she was walking in with Katie. They immediately stopped walking and stared at me. I just smiled back at them. Katie was about to say something when the last bell rang. Thank goodness!

The minute Mr. Grey walked into the room,

I couldn't think of anything else. He was wearing a blue sweater that matched his eyes exactly. With his black pants and cowboy boots, he really looked great. And to think that he was my secret admirer — it was too much. My heart started beating fast. I took a couple of deep breaths to calm myself down.

It was ten minutes into class, and we were in the middle of ancient Greek and Roman history. Winslow and I had raised our hands for the first six questions, and Mr. Grey had picked me four times! I realized that sitting next to Winslow wasn't so bad after all. Winslow raises his hand every time a teacher asks a question, so Mr. Grey was always looking at our side of the room.

"What were some of the contributions that the ancient Greeks and Romans made to modern civilization?" Mr. Grey asked. "Sabrina?"

"Many of the ideas for democracy came from that period," I answered. "Also, people really started to study science and mathematics back then."

"Good! Now can anyone give me an explanation of the democracy that Sabrina was talking about?"

When my hand shot up to answer that question, too, Mr. Grey motioned for me to put it down. Then he leaned back on the front of the desk, folded his arms across his chest, and waited. He looked so cool when he did that. He just stood there and didn't say anything for a few minutes. Finally he spoke.

"Well, guys, since it appears that no one finds talking about ancient Roman history as interesting as Winslow and Sabrina...maybe you'd rather write about it?"

Groans filled the classroom. So much for keeping a low profile! I could feel everyone staring at Winslow and me like they wanted to kill us. My face turned beet red, and I was too embarrassed to look around. Winslow didn't seem to care, though. He just took out a notebook and started clicking one of his pens.

"Don't blame Sabs and Winslow," Mr. Grey continued. "I want to see a summary of either chapter nine, 'Ancient Rome,' or chapter ten, 'Ancient Greece.' You have your choice."

Then Mr. Grey looked straight at me and winked. I thought I was going to die. First he used my nickname in class — and now he was winking at me! I wasn't sure what to do, so I nervously winked back. Then he gave me this big smile. Now I knew I was going to faint.

Everyone started working and the room got really quiet. Suddenly I felt a tap on my shoulder. It was the girl behind me, Florence Norton. She passed me a note without even looking at me. Since there was a lot of giggling coming from the back, I guessed it was probably from Randy and Katie.

Dear Sabs,

You and Winslow look great together, but don't you think Jason is going to be jealous?

K & R

Give me a break! How could they think that I liked Winslow? This whole thing about the secret admirer was turning out to be a mess. I was sure Mr. Grey was the one who'd left the note, but everyone else thought I liked Winslow — even two of my best friends! I had spent half the night waiting for this class to start, and now I couldn't wait for it to end. What a disaster! I handed in my assignment and was just starting to pack up my books when Mr. Grey came over to my desk.

"Sabrina, I just wanted you to know how proud I am of you. You're doing excellent work!" he said, smiling. If his eyes had been green, he would have looked just like Tom Cruise.

"Th-thanks," I stammered.

"Do you think you'd mind staying for a few more minutes? There's something I want to talk to you about," he said.

All the blood drained from my face when he said that. I must have looked as white as a marshmallow. I felt like my heart had stopped beating altogether. Then I did the dumbest thing. I took a deep breath and puffed out my cheeks, and all this air started blowing out of my mouth.

"Sabrina, are you all right?" Mr. Grey asked, looking concerned. "There's nothing wrong. I just wanted to talk to you about a special project...but we can do it tomorrow. There's no rush."

Here I was, face-to-face with my secret admirer, and I couldn't get a word out of my mouth. I just stared at him and nodded. I took another deep breath, and my cheeks puffed up again. I must have looked like a blowfish!

"Sabrina, let's talk about this tomorrow," he suggested. "Go on. You'll be late for your next class." I walked toward the door like a zombie in a monster movie, not even looking where I was going.

What a jerk I had been! Mr. Grey had asked to talk to me, and I'd ruined the whole thing with my blowfish imitation. I dropped the blazer off in my locker. I couldn't wait to get rid of it. It reminded me of that awful class, and of how everyone thought I liked Winslow. The last thing I felt like doing was walking around looking like Winslow's clone.

But I felt a lot better when I remembered what Mr. Grey had said to me and how he had looked. First he had wanted to talk to me about something — probably the note — and then he had looked really worried about me. That must have meant that he cared. I was so excited that I just floated through eighth period. Then I sort of drifted over to Fitzie's, where I was supposed to meet Katie, Randy, and Allison. I couldn't wait to tell them about Mr. Grey.

Then I remembered that my horoscope had said to *guard your secrets carefully* today. And if Mr. Grey was my *secret* admirer, I decided that it would be better if I kept the whole thing to myself for a while.

When I got to Fitzie's, Katie, Randy, and Al were already sitting in one of the booths, and a waitress was just taking their orders. I sat down with them and ordered a root-beer float with vanilla ice cream.

"So, Sabrina," Randy said as soon as the waitress left, "did you and Winslow plan your outfits together, or did he run home and change as soon as he saw your blazer?"

"You make a cute couple," Katie said, giggling.

"Sabrina, aren't those shoes just a little bit too big for you?" Allison asked with a gentle smile. I could tell that they were all just joking, but I pretended to get angry anyway.

"I can't believe this. I thought you guys were my friends." I tried to look hurt. "I got all dressed up today, and all you can do is make fun of me."

Katie and Randy tried to hold back their laughter, and Allison was biting her lip to keep from smiling. So when I looked up with a grin, all four of us just started laughing hysterically.

I was putting the first spoonful of ice cream into my mouth when I caught sight of Stacy

Hansen and Eva Malone heading our way.

"Don't look now," I warned everybody. "Here comes Stacy the Great and her best clone."

Fitzie's is pretty big, and it was absolutely packed full of kids. But Stacy, with her long, wavy blond hair and sea-green jumpsuit, stood out from the crowd. Stacy's friend Eva Malone was following right behind her, as usual, trying to look and act just like Stacy. She was wearing a powder-blue sweater dress that's exactly like one Stacy has, but her brown hair and braces kind of ruined the effect.

"Hello, Sabrina," Stacy said in her creepy voice as she flicked her hair over her shoulder. "Somebody told me that you had a terrific new blazer that I just had to see. What happened to it?"

"She probably had to give it back to Winslow," Eva Malone put in loudly. My brother Sam and his friends call her Jaws, because of her braces. I think it suits her perfectly.

I did my best to ignore them, concentrating on my float. But the two of them wanted to make sure that the entire room heard what they had to say.

"Winslow?" Stacy asked Eva, pretending to be surprised. "What does Winslow have to do with Sabrina's blazer?"

"Sabrina and Winslow really like each other," Eva explained. "In fact, I think Sabrina has a big crush on him. They were wearing the exact same blazer today."

"So," Stacy cooed, "Sabrina has a crush on Winslow. Isn't that sweet!"

That did it. I could only take so much of Stacy, and she had just reached the limit. I stood up, hands on my hips, and glared at Stacy and Eva. "I do not have a crush on Winslow Barton," I said loudly, gritting my teeth. I felt as if everyone in the room was staring at us.

"You don't have to be afraid to tell us that you love Winslow. Your secret is safe with us." Stacy said in a fake, sugary voice. She obviously didn't believe me, and she wanted everyone else to know that she didn't, too.

"If Sabrina said she doesn't, then she doesn't!" Randy said, pointing her finger in Stacy's face.

"Yeah," said Katie and Allison from beside me.

"Oh, I get it," Stacy said sarcastically. "They wore the same clothes today so that everyone would see how much they *don't* like each other, right?"

"No! I mean…yes! I mean…" I was so mad and so worried that everyone would think I really did have a crush on Winslow, I couldn't even think of what to say. I could feel my body blush starting up again.

"You see," Stacy sang out, pointing at me. "All I had to do was mention Winslow's name and she turned bright red. That proves it."

"Sabrina Wells has a major crush on Winslow Barton," Eva Malone chanted.

"Take a hike, bean brain," Randy told Stacy.

"It was just an accident they wore the same blazers today, " Katie said.

"Sure," Stacy said again. She turned around and walked back toward her booth at the other end of Fitzie's.

"Hey, everybody!" Eva Malone called to their booth as she followed Stacy. "Did you hear? Sabrina Wells has a crush on Winslow Barton!" All the kids at the tables around us — most of them from Bradley — heard her loud and clear. They were all talking about it! By tomorrow everyone at Bradley would have heard that I, Sabrina Wells, had a crush on Winslow Barton, class nerd.

I sat down in my chair and stared at the root-beer float that had looked so good just a couple of minutes before. I couldn't even think of touching it now.

"Sabrina?" Katie asked softly. "Are you okay?"

I just shook my head. I would never be okay again. In less than five minutes, Stacy the Great had ruined my entire life.

Chapter Five

I spent most of the night worrying. I was worried about Stacy and the huge rumor she had started. And I was still thinking about how I'd made a fool of myself in front of Mr. Grey. I also decided that the older, more sophisticated look, namely the plaid blazer, just wasn't me. Besides, Mr. Grey obviously liked me just the way I was. So I decided to go back to wearing my regular clothes.

In order to prevent my blowfish problem from happening the next time I spoke to Mr. Grey, I tried to come up with some good lines of conversation. I just got so flustered when he talked to me, I couldn't think of anything to say. I decided that I should have at least three different topics of conversation planned.

I sat on my bed with a pad and pencil in my lap and thought about it. I had tons of home work to do, but I just couldn't stop daydreaming. I wrote a list of topics in my notebook. Number one, I would ask him to tell me more about ancient Greek and Roman history. Thinking about ancient Greek and Roman history made me think of those movies they show on cable TV all the time. That made me think about how much Mr. Grey looked like a movie star. Then before you knew it, I was imagining Mr. Grey as the star of a movie about ancient Greece and Rome.

Movies! Great! That would be subject number two. I would ask Mr. Grey to name his favorite movie. I pictured him telling me about his collection of famous movies that were all on videocassette, just like those TV ads. Then I imagined him telling me that he watched his absolute favorite *favorite* movie only on his birthday. Great! Then I could ask him about his birthday. That way, I could find out whether or not he was an Aquarius.

And the last topic would of course be all about him. I heard this lady on a talk show once say that men love to talk about themselves. All of the magazines say that the best way to show a guy that you like him, is to show interest in the things he likes. This was turning out to be very good. I could ask him why he became a teacher. No, first I'd say, "Mr. Grey, you're the best teacher I've ever had." Then I'd ask him why he became a teacher.

Three questions. That should do it. At least I wouldn't sound like such a bingo head next time. Why hadn't I thought of this before? I would really impress him with my intelligent conversation. I was so excited I didn't think I could wait for school in the morning!

When I woke up the next morning, I just knew that I had been dreaming about Mr. Grey. It's a proven fact that if you concentrate on something before you go to sleep, you can make yourself dream about the last thing in your mind before you go to sleep. The only thing that I could remember about the dream was that we had been fishing for blowfish off the coast of ancient Greece. Anyway, it made me wake up in an incredibly great mood. I got ready for school in record time and grabbed Section C of the newspaper on my way out the door.

Naturally, since I was looking forward to something, the whole day dragged by. It took forever just to get to lunch! I was really excited because I'd read my horoscope prediction on the way to school, and it had said: *Your charisma impresses someone. The bloom of love will present itself in the form of a small gift.* I just knew that Mr. Grey was going to be impressed with my intelligence today. Even Stacy Hansen's rumors that I like-*liked* Winslow Barton couldn't ruin my mood, although I could tell people were whispering about me and Winslow all day.

When it was finally time for social studies, I almost ran from my sixth period class. The moment I got into class, Mr. Grey called me up to his desk at the front of the room.

"Sabrina, make sure you stay after class today," he said. "I've got something special in mind for you."

"Sure, Mr. Grey," I replied, batting my eyelashes at him. He gave me a strange look when I did that. I warned myself to chill out as I walked back to my regular seat next to Katie and Randy. I guess it wouldn't have been very cool for him to show his feelings for me in front of the whole class. I decided I'd better calm down and wait until later.

Then Mr. Grey did something that really

blew my mind. He asked Florence Norton to stay after class, too! What was that supposed to mean? Now I was getting worried. How could Mr. Grey and I talk if Florence was in the room with us? I spent the entire period trying to figure out what was going on.

Finally it dawned on me. Florence Norton was just part of the cover-up. I mean, how would it look for Mr. Grey to single me out? He was probably going to say something to Florence about her homework and then send her off to class so that he could talk to me privately. Wow! He was so smart!

It seemed like hours but finally the period was over. I packed my books and waited for the room to clear out. But it didn't! Florence, Katie, Winslow, and six other kids were all sitting at their desks and waiting for Mr. Grey, too.

"What's this all about?" Katie whispered to me.

"I don't know," I answered. "When did he ask you to stay after?"

"Just before class," Katie replied. "He said he had a special project for me."

Oh, great, I thought. Maybe there really was

a special project. This was probably not going to be the moment when my secret admirer would reveal his identity. The next ten minutes went by in a sort of blur. Mr. Grey told us that there were visitors from the Board of Education coming to Bradley the following Monday. He had decided to pick ten of his best students to put together a presentation for them. Mr. Grey went on to explain that we would be divided into teams. Each team would be assigned a specific period in history, and we were supposed to write a little skit and perform it.

I was really bummed. As usual, I had gotten carried away by my imagination. But then a thought struck me. This could be my chance — the perfect opportunity to impress Mr. Grey with my acting talent. Now I was starting to love the whole idea. Then Mr. Grey told us that he had already picked the teams. I hoped I would get lucky and end up with Katie. I almost died, though, when he called out my partner's name.

"And since Sabrina and Winslow have demonstrated such an avid interest in ancient Greek and Roman history, they'll be team

number five," he announced. Winslow Barton!
I couldn't believe my ears. Me and my big
mouth — answering all those questions had
gotten me into this. This project was going to
ruin my life. I tried not to make a face — especially when Winslow turned around and gave
me a big stupid smile. I flashed him a fake little grin, realizing that I was going to have to
make the best of it.

Finally we were dismissed. I decided to
hang around for a while, getting my stuff
together really slowly and keeping my fingers
crossed that Mr. Grey would have something
else to say to me. I told Katie I'd catch up with
her later. I stood by my desk and pretended to
be looking through my notes.

"Anything wrong, Sabrina?" Mr. Grey finally asked, looking up from the papers he was
going through at his desk.

"No, no," I casually replied in a deeper-
than-usual voice, trying to show how mature I
really was despite my age.

"Then shouldn't you be off to your next
class?" he asked.

"I guess so," I answered in an even lower
voice, batting my eyelashes and looking into

his deep blue eyes.

"Do you have a cold, Sabrina?" Mr. Grey asked me suddenly.

"No, why?" I answered in surprise.

"Your voice sounds a little funny, that's all," Mr. Grey said. "There's a lot of flu going around."

Well, so much for the voice, I thought. It absolutely was not working.

"Do you have any questions about the project?" he continued.

"Well...n-no," I answered. My mind was turning to mush. I didn't know what to say. All I knew was that I should get out of there — soon. But my feet stayed glued to the floor. "Mr. Grey?" I began hesitantly in my regular voice.

"Yes," he answered, looking up from his papers again.

"Have you ever been to the movies?" I asked quickly.

"Yes, of course," he replied, sounding confused.

Now my mind was blank. *You're supposed to be making conversation,* I reminded myself. I had to ask him another question. I looked at his dark, wavy hair, and all I could think about was my daydream. "Mr. Grey?"

"Yes, Sabrina," he answered, smiling. "Is there something else you wanted to ask me?"

Now I was a bowl of Jell-O. Mr. Grey was looking straight at me. My knees started to buckle. My mouth felt as if it was full of cotton balls. The right words were in my head, but they were all jumbled up. Something told me that I should just say good-bye, but I couldn't help myself. "Um, yes, Mr. Grey. I wanted to know if you've ever had a birthday."

"Of course," he answered, giving me an odd look. "I've been to the movies *and* I've had a birthday. Is there anything else I can help you with?"

"Uh...are you a teacher?" I asked.

"Am I a teacher?" he repeated, raising his eyebrows and looking very confused. "Well, yes, Sabrina. I guess that's why you're here in school, talking to me."

"Yeah," I agreed, taking a deep breath. "That's probably *why* you're a teacher. Because you're so smart, I mean."

"Well, thank you for saying that, Sabrina. Now I think you had better get going. The bell's going to ring any minute now."

"Yeah. You're right," I said, heading for the door. "See you tomorrow." I waved, tripping over a chair in the aisle.

"Watch your step, Sabrina," Mr. Grey warned. "I wouldn't want anything to happen to you."

"See you tomorrow," I repeated, recovering my balance. He just nodded his head and went back to his papers.

I walked as quickly as I could to the bathroom. Thank goodness there was no one else there. I splashed my face with cold water to stop myself from blushing, then stared at myself in the mirror. "Have you been to the movies?" I asked my reflection. "Have you had a birthday?" How could I have asked those questions? Mr. Grey must have thought I was a real nut case.

I left the bathroom and headed to study hall, replaying our conversation over and over in my mind. I couldn't believe how ridiculously I had acted. As I sat down at a table in the library, I realized that nothing even the teeniest bit positive had come of my big chat with Mr. Grey. Then I remembered the last thing he had said: "I wouldn't want anything to happen to you." He wouldn't have said that unless he meant it. Maybe Mr. Grey was really shy or something. Maybe he was afraid to tell me how he felt when we were actually face-to-face. Maybe that was why he had written the note!

Poor, shy Mr. Grey, I thought as I wrote his name in my notebook. I would just have to wait until he built up his courage to talk to me. I was so caught up in thinking about him that it took a while for me to notice that the bell had rung and nearly everyone was already gone. I picked up my books and walked toward my locker to get my coat and everything I needed to do my homework.

Suddenly I felt a tap on my shoulder. It was Randy.

"Guess who's looking for you," she said with a sly smile, interrupting my thoughts.

"Winslow Barton, right?" I answered quickly.

"How did you guess?" she said, laughing.

"I just had a feeling," I replied. My luck had been so bad most of the day that it just figured that Winslow was looking for me. After all, he was the last person on Earth I wanted to see.

"So it looks like you two were meant to be together," Randy teased.

"Who? Me and Winslow?" I asked, shocked. "Would you give me a break?"

"I'm just kidding," she said with a laugh. "He was going to show me a music program on his computer after school, but he said that the two of you had to work on this special history project. He asked me to find out if you wanted to get started today. If you do, you can come with me."

Actually it sounded like a good idea. At least Randy would be there. And Winslow and I only had until Monday to do the whole special project. And we had to do an incredible job on it, since it was for...Mr. Grey.

"Okay," I answered.

"I'll meet you back here in two minutes, okay?" Randy said.

"Okay," I agreed.

"Ciao," Randy called as she walked down the hallway.

I had opened up my locker and was looking for my English notebook when I noticed a pink envelope taped to the inside of the locker door. It was the same size envelope and the same exact pink as the other one. It had to be another note from my secret admirer! My heart started beating really quickly. I carefully pulled the pink envelope off the door. My name was written clearly on the front — SABRINA WELLS.

I held the envelope, thinking about all the time Mr. Grey must have spent thinking about what he wanted to say. I sighed and turned the note over to open it. There was the same little red heart sticker on the flap. But this time there was a message written above it — *Do not open until you look on the top shelf.*

I stood on my tiptoes and reached up, feeling around for whatever might be there. My fingers touched something long and skinny. I pulled down a couple of roses wrapped in that kind of clear plastic the florists use. I just stood there for a minute with my mouth hanging open in surprise. The flowers were absolutely beautiful. Actually they were kind of wilted from sitting in my locker without water, but they were the prettiest flowers I'd ever seen. After all, they were from my secret admirer.

The flowers reminded me of something, but

for a second I couldn't figure out what. Then I remembered — my horoscope had predicted this! The *bloom of love* was supposed to take the form of a *small gift*. And Mr. Grey had given me flowers!

I quickly hid the flowers in my knapsack. Then I slowly and carefully opened the envelope. I didn't want to tear it, since I planned to keep it for the rest of my life. I took a deep breath and read the note. It began just like the last one:

> *My Dear Sabrina,*
>> *Roses are red,*
>> *Violets are blue.*
>> *You deserve a gift of diamonds,*
>> *But these will have to do.*
>>> *Love,*
>>> *Your Secret Admirer*

A love poem, I thought with a sigh. How romantic can you get? Suddenly, someone banged on my locker door. I crammed the note into my pocket. Shoot! Now it was going to be all wrinkled.

"Hey, let's go!" Randy said loudly, her skateboard tucked under her arm. "I told Winslow that we'd be at his house by three-thirty. If we don't hurry, we're going to be late."

"I'm coming," I replied, smiling. gathering my things and following her down the hall. I decided to wait until later to tell her about the flowers. I didn't want her to mention them in front of Winslow.

Chapter Six

I don't know what I expected Winslow's house to be like. Something out of a science-fiction movie, I guess. But the Bartons lived in an ordinary two-story house, painted yellow, with a porch in front and a garage on one side.

As we walked up the front steps something strange happened. It was just like one of those horror movies that Randy and her mom like. The door opened all the way, but there was nobody to be seen. We stepped into the foyer.

"BOO!" Winslow shouted, jumping out from behind the door. I couldn't believe it. He was in his own house and he was still wearing one of his dumb blazers. It had a horrible navy-blue background with gray stripes running through it. I could remember him wearing it back in the fifth grade at Acorn Elementary. Now the sleeves were too short.

"I've been vaiting for you ladies," Winslow

announced, using this dumb Dracula voice. "Velcome to my home."

"I don't know if I'm going to make it through this project," I whispered to Randy.

"Oh, he's just kidding," Randy replied, nudging me with her elbow. "Chill out, Sabrina. Really."

"Let me show you to my la-bor-a-tory," Winslow continued, leading the way to his dad's study. His dad works for a really big computer corporation. I heard my dad tell my mom that Mr. Barton is a real genius. You can tell just by looking at his house. There were all kinds of video equipment, a huge stereo system, a ham radio setup, and two computers — one for Winslow and one for his dad. Every wall was covered with shelves, some holding books but most full of tapes, computer disks, records, and CDs. The Bartons seemed to have more equipment than furniture!

Set up on its own stand in the corner by the window was a huge fish tank. It was filled with the weirdest fish I'd ever seen. The tank was octagonal and had tan stones on the bottom, and plants — real ones, not the plastic kind — growing in it. There were some black-spotted white fish that looked like they had just fins and no bodies. There were a whole group of tiny fish with electric-blue and red stripes on them. On the bottom of the tank something that looked like a pile of worms was wiggling all over the place. There were lots of other fish swimming around, too. It was kind of gross but kind of cool at the same time.

Winslow took out a big plastic box full of computer disks.

"Here's the music program I was telling you about," he said, handing Randy a disk and a thick manual. "I'll set it up for you so you can play around with it."

Winslow sat down in front of the computer and expertly started up the program. Soon he was playing little bits and pieces of different songs as he showed Randy what to do. He stood up to give Randy the chance to try it out, then waited to see if she had any questions. I thought that was really nice of him.

"Do either of you want a snack?" Winslow asked. "My mom just baked some brownies this afternoon."

"Awesome!" exclaimed Randy, not even looking up from her manual.

"Brownies are my favorite," I added.

"I'll be right back," said Winslow, and he ran out of the room. While I waited, I started putting my social studies notes in order. It was funny, but I had a lot more pages covered with Mr. Grey's name than pages of actual notes. I also checked to make sure my flowers were still there. They were a little crushed from being in my knapsack, but they still smelled great.

"I hope you guys like chocolate," Winslow said, coming through the door with a huge tray. He had brought a big pile of brownies and some sodas. "Sabrina, I brought you a diet cola, since I know you like those better."

"Thanks, Winslow," I said, surprised. "How did you know I like diet soda?"

"Oh, I just knew," he said. For some reason his ears started to turn pink. "Why don't we get started on the project?"

"Sure," I replied. "Do you have any ideas for the skit?"

"Well, I was thinking that we could do a sort of time trick and pretend that a person from ancient Rome ran into a person from ancient Greece."

"Hey, that's a good idea," I told him. "That way each of us could ask all kinds of questions about the other person's time period. We could compare them."

"Right," Winslow said and nodded. "I think we can include a lot of information that way."

"We sure can," I agreed. "What else do you think we should do?"

"Well, I think that the most effective way to illustrate the way in which the ancient Greeks and Romans lived would be for the two of us to wear togas," Winslow continued.

I had been getting pretty excited about Winslow's ideas for our project, but togas were a bit much. "Togas?" I asked him. "Are you sure that's a good idea?"

"Absolutely," Winslow replied, pushing his glasses back up on his nose.

"Winslow, I don't care what else you ask me to do for this project," I said seriously, "but I am not going to get up in front of the entire class wearing nothing but a sheet," I told him firmly.

"Well, then what do you propose we wear?" he asked calmly .

I sighed heavily. It was just like Winslow to put it that way — "What do you propose we wear?" See, that's one of the reasons everyone calls him a nerd. He always sounds like a text-book.

"I *propose*," I began, "that we just wear our regular clothes."

"No way, Sabrina," he said. "If we're going to do this, let's make it authentic."

I sighed. "Winslow, have you memorized the entire dictionary?"

"No," he replied very seriously. "I've only read up to the letter *M* so far."

"Winslow has a photographic memory, Sabs," Randy cut in, looking up from the computer. "All he has to do is read something once and he knows it by heart."

"Is there anything wrong with using the English language to its fullest extent?" Winslow asked.

"You know, Winslow — " I began.

"Why don't you two go somewhere else and fight," Randy interrupted. "I can't concentrate on this thing with you two blabbing away."

We slowly gathered our things and moved

into the living room. We put our books on the coffee table and sat down on the floor.

"What were you about to say?" Winslow asked, crossing his arms on the table. I just stared at him. I didn't know what I had been about to say. "Well?" he said, waiting for me to go on.

"Well...nothing," I said grumpily. "I'm just not going to wear a toga. It's too embarrassing. Everyone will laugh. Can't we just use pictures or something?"

"Togas will be much more realistic," he said. "Besides, there's nothing to be embarrassed about."

"Everyone will laugh," I repeated.

"So?" he said. "What's the big deal?"

"*So?*" I repeated. "Do you have any idea how humiliating it would be to have all those people laughing at us? And they would tell everyone in the whole school about how Winslow Barton and Sabrina Wells wore sheets to school, and..."

"Sabrina," Winslow said quietly, pushing his glasses up again, "it doesn't make any difference to me what all those kids think. And it shouldn't matter to you, either."

"Of course it matters to me!" I shouted at him. "If every kid in the whole school was making fun of me all the time, I would just... just...die!"

Winslow didn't say anything. He had pulled his pocket protector out of his pocket and was playing with it, rearranging the pens. Looking at that pocket protector, I thought about what I had just said.

"You really *wouldn't* care if they laughed, would you?" I said quietly. Winslow kept rearranging his pens. "The kids at school are always making fun of you, but it doesn't matter to you what they say or think."

"It used to," he said shyly. "But my mom says that lots of really great people, like inventors and scientists and musicians, were great because they were different from everybody else. And it was hard for them because nobody understood them."

I nodded. I hadn't really paid much attention to Winslow before because I thought he was a nerd — you know, really smart and always talking about math and science. But he seemed like a really nice, interesting person. I guess nobody else knew that, either — nobody except for Randy. Randy thinks it's good to be different from other people.

"Everyone already thinks I'm the class nerd, so I figure my reputation can't get any worse, can it?" Winslow asked with a smile.

"Listen, about the toga — " I started.

"Think of it this way," Winslow interrupted. "We're doing this project to help Mr. Grey. How would it look if I played a Roman in a toga and you were wearing a pink miniskirt or something?"

"Mr. Grey!" I exclaimed. "That's right. I guess he'd be pretty upset if I messed up the presentation in front of the guests. Okay, Winslow," I agreed. "I'll wear a toga."

"Great!" Winslow replied.

"On one condition," I added.

"What's that?" he asked.

"That I get to wear a leotard underneath." I wanted to be sure I'd have something on just in case my toga slipped.

"Okay," he agreed, grinning. "That sounds fair. Rad-some!" he exclaimed with a satisfied look on his face. One thing Winslow does that drives everyone crazy is take all the cool words that everyone uses and mix them up into new words. Like *rad-some*. That's a combination of *radical* and *awesome*.

"We'd better get to work on this project," I told him.

A little later, while Winslow was writing down some of our ideas, I started thinking about the flowers I'd gotten from my secret admirer. I reached into my pocket and touched the crumpled piece of notepaper. I really loved the poem and the flowers, but it would be so much nicer if Mr. Grey would *tell* me how he felt instead of writing about it. I wondered if there was something I could do to help him get over being shy. Guys are so hard to figure out, though. You probably have to be one to actually understand the way they think.

Wait a minute! I sure couldn't be a boy, but at least I could ask one. Maybe Winslow could tell me what to do about my secret admirer being so shy. I wouldn't really tell him about Mr. Grey. I would just sort of give him a vague idea so I could get his opinion. I'd have to be careful, though, not to say the wrong thing.

"Winslow," I started slowly, "have you ever liked somebody? I mean, have you ever had a crush on anyone?"

Winslow suddenly dropped his pen and it bounced off the coffee table and onto the rug. He reached down to grab for it. "Yeah," he muttered. "I guess so."

"Did you tell her?"

"Tell her what?" he asked.

"That you liked her," I explained patiently.

Winslow hesitated. I noticed that his ears had turned pink again. Was Winslow Barton blushing? How cute! Winslow must have a crush on someone!

"No, not exactly," he said finally.

"Were you worried about what she would do if you told her? That maybe she wouldn't like you as much as you liked her?" I tried not to sound too eager, but I was anxious to see if he could help me.

"Yes. No. I don't know!" Winslow sounded upset and his ears were the brightest shade of red I'd ever seen. "Why are we talking about this, anyway?" he asked.

I decided to pretend that it wasn't really that important to me. "No reason," I said, waving my hand in the air. "I was just curious. I was wondering why guys sometimes decide to write love letters and stuff instead of telling a girl how they feel in person. What do you think?"

"I think," said Winslow slowly, taking a deep breath, "that we're supposed to be working on our history project...which is due on Monday, if I may remind you. Come on, Sabrina. We don't have a lot of time. Let's get started on the script."

"All right," I agreed, digging into my knapsack for some more paper. "Let's get going." So much for a man's point of view. *But it didn't really matter*, I thought as I sneaked another peek at my flowers. As long as I kept reading my horoscope I'd know what to do next.

"Hey, you two," Randy said, coming into the living room. "It's getting kind of late. Sabs and I should probably go home."

"Wow! I didn't realize how much time had gone by, " I said, looking at my watch. I gathered up all my papers and put them into my knapsack, making sure I didn't crush the flowers.

"That's a really cool program, Winslow," Randy remarked. "It gave me some great ideas for a new song."

"I knew you'd like it," Winslow said, grinning. "We came up with some pretty good ideas, too."

"It's going to be a great skit, Ran," I put in. Then I turned to Winslow. "Thanks for the brownies and soda, Winslow. I'll finish writing my scene, and we'll get together on Saturday to practice. Okay?"

"Sure," he agreed.

"So," said Randy as soon as the door was closed behind us. "Did you and Winslow get along okay after I threw you out of the den?"

"Yeah, we did," I answered. "He really is a pretty interesting guy once you get past the blazers." We laughed, walking up the street toward the corner. "He even talked me into wearing a toga for our presentation."

"Now *that* I've got to see," Randy said and laughed.

We reached the corner where I had to turn to go home, and we said good-bye. I ran the rest of the way so I would make it in time for dinner. All the while I was thinking about tall, dark, gorgeous, shy Mr. Grey. I decided to work really hard writing that scene for our presentation. I'd work on it tonight, tomorrow, and Saturday and Sunday, too, if I had to.

Usually, I hate doing homework, but this was for Mr. Grey.

Chapter Seven

According to my horoscope, Friday was supposed to be *quiet, calm, and uneventful*, and I was supposed to *spend the day in contemplation and away from stressful situations*. It turned out to be the longest day I'd ever had. We had a substitute for social studies, so I didn't even get a chance to see Mr. Grey. I had fun after school, though. We went over to Katie's house and watched TV for a while. I told everyone about the flowers and the poem. I could tell they were impressed — even Randy.

On Saturday morning, I got up early to finish my chores before I went to Winslow's house. I was feeling a little grumpy because that morning my horoscope had been kind of on the negative side: *Disturbing news prevents you from being your happy-go-lucky self. Don't feel sorry for yourself. Use your imagination*. I just kept hoping that the disturbing news wouldn't have anything to do with Mr. Grey.

When I got to Winslow's house, I could see him through the window. He was working at his computer. *Probably typing his homework*, I thought. I rang the bell. It took a while for him to answer it. When he did, I understood why. He was wearing his toga and a crown of leaves around his head. I couldn't help laughing. He looked so funny.

"Like my outfit?" Winslow asked, turning around slowly. Secretly, I had to admit, it did look pretty neat. "My mom helped me with the toga. And she made one for you, too. I figured that we'd work on your crown after we finish our script. I was just typing it into the computer."

"You look really cool," I said, stepping inside. "You sure have been working hard on this project."

"Well, if we're going to do it, we might as well do it right," he announced, leading me into the study. It was a typical Winslow saying. He was always coming up with corny things like that. But I had to admit there was usually something to those corny sayings.

"I finished scene one. How far did you get

with scene two?" he asked.

"It's all done," I said, fishing it out of my bag. I had worked on it for hours on Thursday night and Friday after school, trying to put in everything we had learned about the ancient Greeks and Romans. I was pretty happy with it.

"Why don't you read mine and I'll read yours, and then we'll compare notes," I suggested.

"Sounds fair," he agreed, settling into his desk chair. I sat down in front of Mr. Barton's desk and started reading.

Winslow's script was very good, of course. He had added a lot of interesting facts about everyday life in ancient Greece and Rome. And he said he liked my script, too. That made me feel really good. All we had to do was put them together in a way that made sense. After what seemed like a short time, I looked at my watch. It turned out that we had been working for two hours.

"Wow! Look at the time," I exclaimed. "I can't believe we've been working so long."

"And I can't believe we're almost finished," Winslow commented. "Time sure flies when you're having fun."

"You know, this *has* been fun," I agreed, ignoring another corny Winslow saying. "It's getting late today, but we should probably get together and practice one more time before the presentation."

"Hey, that's a great idea, Sabrina," exclaimed Winslow. "Why don't you come over tomorrow afternoon and we'll run through the whole thing?"

"Excellent!" I said, and we shook hands.

"All this work has certainly given me an appetite," I continued, motioning toward the kitchen.

"I'm hungry, too," Winslow agreed. "Why don't you type out these last two pages while I get some chips and soda."

"Sounds good to me," I replied, taking the notebook he held out. I waited until he had gone and then took his notebook over to the computer, where I had seen a box of tissues. I put the notebook down on top of the pile of books we had been using and reached for the box. I bumped my arm against one of the books and half of the pile slid to the floor.

"What a pain," I muttered under my breath

as I got down on my hands and knees to straighten up the mess. There were scraps of notes and loose papers all over the place. I picked them up one by one, trying to put them in order. I couldn't believe all the notes Winslow took! It looked as if he wrote down every word the teachers said. Since he usually typed everything, I was surprised to see what nice handwriting he had. There was something very familiar about it. I laughed, thinking about my notes. Half the time I didn't even understand what I had written.

As I picked up the books that had fallen, one of them opened and a couple of sheets of paper fell out — pink paper. My heart stopped as I picked them up and looked at them. I couldn't believe what I read! *My Dear Sabrina,* the first one said. *I can't stop thinking about you. You are like a beautiful star...* The word *star* was crossed out and replaced with the word *moon.* Then *moon* was scratched out and replaced with the word *flower.* I turned the book upside down and shook it out. Just as I had suspected, a week's worth of horoscope predictions floated out and into a pile on the floor. Copies of my love notes were all over the place. Now everything was beginning to make sense. My secret admirer wasn't Mr. Grey at all! It was just Winslow playing some kind of joke on me! I thought about all of the stupid things I had done to try to impress Mr. Grey and if I hadn't been so angry, I would have cried. I could hear Winslow's footsteps coming back down the hall.

"Break time," he said as he walked into the room. When he saw me glaring at him with the love notes in my hand, he stopped in his tracks. The glasses of soda he was carrying wiggled on the tray. One tipped over and sent diet cola spilling all over the rug. Winslow didn't even try to mop it up. He just stared at the floor and didn't say a word. His ears turned bright pink.

"How could you do this, Winslow?" I yelled, holding a fistful of papers in each hand. "How could you do this to *me*?"

"Sabrina...I..."

"I can't believe that you were the one who wrote all those notes. Why did you do it?" I shouted. I felt the tears starting to well up in my eyes. I kept thinking about what a fool I had made out of myself in front of Mr. Grey.

"Well?" I demanded.

Winslow looked up. "I'm really sorry, Sabrina," he said miserably. "I never meant to hurt you. It was Sam's idea."

"Sam's idea?" I asked. "Sam! Did you say Sam?" By now I was screaming.

"He said it was just a practical joke," Winslow explained, looking desperate. "He said that he wanted to show you how silly horoscope predictions are."

"I don't believe this!" I yelled.

"I'm sorry, Sabrina. Really," Winslow quietly apologized. "I never would have done it if I thought it would bother you. Sam said you'd think it was funny. He said that it was just a joke."

"Well, I don't think it's funny at all," I told him as I grabbed my coat and bag and stormed out of the house. I was so sick of hearing Sam say *"It was just a joke, it was just a joke."* The words were flying around in my head. He'd said them when he squirted me with the hose last Saturday. He'd said them again when he messed up my sleepover and left me standing there in my bathing cap. I was getting angrier by the second.

Suddenly the words from today's horoscope prediction flashed through my mind.
*Don't feel sorry for yourself. Use your imagina-
tion.* Then I remembered reading something in
Madame Pandora's book. *The Pisces personality
takes advantage of every opportunity.* I felt like a
character in a cartoon with one of those light
bulbs above my head to show that I'd just had
a great idea. Enough of Sam's tricks and practical jokes! Now it was my turn to get even! By
the time I finished with Sam, he wouldn't
know what hit him. *It takes two to tango,* I
thought. Oh, no! Winslow's corny sayings
were beginning to stick.

Chapter Eight

Sabrina calls Katie.

KATIE: Hello?

SABRINA: Katie, it's Sabrina. I've got something important to tell you.

KATIE: What is it?

SABRINA: I just found out who my secret admirer is!

KATIE: You did! Who is it? Quick! Tell me!

SABRINA: Winslow.

KATIE: *Winslow?* Winslow Barton?

SABRINA: Well, actually it was Sam!

KATIE: Did you just say Sam? Sabs, either I'm going crazy or you just told me that your own brother is your secret admirer. What's going on here?

SABRINA: Listen! See, Sam thinks I'm crazy to believe in horoscopes, right?

KATIE: Right.

SABRINA: So he came up with this idea to
            make all of my horoscope predic-
            tions in the newspaper come true.
            He got Winslow to write the
            notes, got my locker combination
            from the desk drawer in my
            room, and started putting the
            notes in the locker.

KATIE: Wow! He sure fooled all of us. So
            what are you going to do now?
            And what about Winslow?

SABRINA: I haven't even thought about
            Winslow yet. But I'm definitely
            going to get Sam back.

KATIE: How?

SABRINA: That's the part I haven't figured
            out yet. I called you because I
            thought we could come up with
            something together. Will you help
            me?

KATIE: I'd love to! Why don't we call
            Allison and Randy, too. They'll
            probably have some great ideas!

SABRINA: Okay! You call Randy, and I'll call
            Allison.

KATIE: I'll call her right now. Talk to you later.

SABRINA: Bye, Katie.

Sabrina calls Allison.

CHARLIE: Are you from Mars?

ALLISON: (in background) Charlie! I told you not to answer the phone. (on phone) Hello. Allison Cloud speaking.

SABRINA: Hi, Al. It's Sabrina.

ALLISON: Hi!

SABRINA: Listen, I need your help. I've got to play a trick on Sam to get him back, and I can't think of what I should do.

ALLISON: Sam must have really done it this time. What did he do?

SABRINA: He made up a secret admirer for me! He got Winslow to write the notes, and Sam put them into my locker himself. He did everything he could to make it seem like my horoscope predictions were coming true.

ALLISON: Well, that explains it. Winslow

wrote the notes? I knew it was
someone shy!

SABRINA: Who cares whether Winslow is
shy or not? I've got to get back at
Sam for this.

ALLISON: Yeah, I guess you do. Have you
come up with any ideas yet?

SABRINA: Well, I was thinking that maybe I
should play a trick on him. You
know, show him how it feels to be
in my shoes for a change.

ALLISON: That's an idea, as long as you
don't do anything too mean.

SABRINA: Nah, I'd never do anything really
mean. Don't worry. But what
kind of trick can I play on him?

ALLISON: Hmm.

SABRINA: Well, I could let all the air out of
his basketball. That would really
make him mad.

ALLISON: But making him mad isn't the
point, is it?

SABRINA: No, but I have to do something to
make him stop doing stuff like
this to me.

ALLISON: Right. You want to teach him a

lesson. So, first of all, you should think about what's important to him.

SABRINA: Something important to him, huh? Well, there's basketball. And our dog, Cinnamon. But I don't think I can do anything with those.

ALLISON: What about Stacy Hansen?

SABRINA: *Stacy Hansen?*

ALLISON: Sure. He has a crush on her, right?

SABRINA: Al, that's the best idea I've ever heard! I've got to tell Randy!

ALLISON: Okay. I'm glad I could help. Good-bye, Sabs.

SABRINA: Bye!

Sabrina calls Randy.

RANDY: Hel-lo!

SABRINA: Randy, it's Sabrina. Have you talked to Katie yet?

RANDY: Yeah, she just hung up. Sam sure pulled a rotten trick on you. I'm glad I don't have any brothers.

SABRINA: You're lucky you don't!

RANDY: So did you come up with a way

	to get Sam back?
SABRINA:	Allison did. See, I wanted to do something to show Sam how it feels to be on the other side of a practical joke, and Allison said it should be about something important to him.
RANDY:	Like what?
SABRINA:	Like Stacy Hansen! He has a crush on her, remember?
RANDY:	Oh, I see! You can do the same thing to him that he did to you!
SABRINA:	Yeah! I'll leave a note in his locker and make him think it's from Stacy.
RANDY:	No, you don't want to do everything the same. That would be too obvious. Why don't you leave it in one of his books or something?
SABRINA:	Yeah, that's even better. Then he won't have any idea what's going on.
RANDY:	And why don't you make it an invitation from Stacy instead of just a letter? You know, have her invite him over to her house for

dinner or something.

SABRINA: And when he knocks on the door she won't even know what he's talking about! I can hardly wait to see his face when he figures it out.

RANDY: This is going to be awesome!

SABRINA: I think I'll ask Winslow to write the note for me. His handwriting is really neat. And he owes me one.

RANDY: He knows calligraphy, too.

SABRINA: Uh-oh. Sam just came in, so I've got to go. I'll talk to you later.

RANDY: Ciao!

One hour later, Sabrina calls Winslow.

WINSLOW: Barton residence. Winslow speaking.

SABRINA: Hi, Winslow, it's Sabrina.

WINSLOW: Sabrina? Is there a problem with the project?

SABRINA: No, the project's all done. I'm still coming over tomorrow to practice with you. This is something else.

WINSLOW: I'm glad you called. I wanted to

tell you how sorry I am about writing those notes for Sam.

SABRINA: Winslow, are you really sorry?

WINSLOW: Of course I am.

SABRINA: Well, I'll forgive you if you do one little thing for me.

WINSLOW: I'll do anything.

SABRINA: All I want you to do is write one little invitation for me. It's for Sam.

WINSLOW: An invitation? For Sam?

SABRINA: Yeah. An invitation to have dinner with Stacy Hansen at her house!

WINSLOW: Sabrina, I don't think that I should get involved. I got into enough trouble writing those notes to you.

SABRINA: Please, Winslow! Sam would recognize my handwriting. I really need your help.

WINSLOW: Well…

SABRINA: Thank you so much! Katie, Randy, and Allison will probably all come with me to your house tomorrow to help us figure out what to write. See you then, Winslow!

WINSLOW: I'll see you tomorrow, Sabrina.

Chapter Nine

Sunday afternoon I met Katie, Randy, and Allison at Winslow's house. We all stood around Winslow's desk and watched him write the fake dinner invitation from Stacy to Sam. He was using his calligraphy pen and some pale yellow stationery that his mother had given him.

"How should I start it?" Winslow asked uncomfortably.

"How about *My Dear Sam*?" I suggested. "You started all of my letters with *My Dear*."

"No, it has to be different from your letters," Randy said.

"How about *Dearest Sam* instead," Allison suggested.

"Okay," I agreed. "*Dearest Sam...*" I couldn't think of anything else to say.

"Tell him that she thinks she really likes him," Katie said.

"And that she wants him to come over for dinner on Friday night," Randy added.

"At six o'clock," I put in.

Winslow started writing:

> *Dearest Sam,*
>
> *I really like you. I would love to have you come over to my house for dinner this Friday night at six o'clock. We'll have a lot of fun. See you then!*
>
> *Stacy*

"Awesome! Stacy could have written that herself," said Randy after Winslow read it aloud to us.

"But suppose Sam mentions it to Stacy before Friday. What happens then?" Winslow asked.

"Oh, no. That would ruin the whole thing!" Katie wailed.

"We could put a P.S. on the bottom," Allison suggested. "Something like *Let's just keep this our little secret.*"

"Good idea," I agreed.

"Yeah. That way he won't mention it to Nick or Jason either," Randy added.

"He wouldn't tell them anyway," Winslow put in as he wrote the last line.

"Probably not," I said. "If Sam knew that Stacy really liked him, he wouldn't want anybody to find out — especially Nick and Jason. They would just make fun of him. Aren't most guys like that, Winslow?"

"I guess so," he said. Then his ears started turning pink again.

From the corner of my eye I saw Katie, Randy, and Allison all give each other these strange looks and smiles. It was as if they were saying "I told you so."

"What do you say, guys?" I asked them. "Do you think it's a good idea to put the invitation in Sam's English book? He and Stacy have English together."

"He'll think Stacy put it there for sure," Katie said, nodding.

Winslow folded the note up carefully and put it in a matching yellow envelope with Sam's name written on the front. I tucked it into one of my books for safekeeping and pulled out my copy of our ancient history script.

"Winslow and I have to rehearse our skit for tomorrow," I told the girls. "Do you want to stay and watch?"

Allison, Katie, and Randy looked at each other again and grinned.

"No, thanks," Randy said. "I've got to go home and clean my room."

"I have to work on my own project," Katie chimed in. "We'll get to see your skit tomorrow."

"And I have to go watch Charlie," Allison added.

All three of them put on their coats, said good-bye, and practically ran out the door. I just shrugged and turned back to Winslow. I didn't have time to wonder what my friends were up to. We had a lot of work to do. With his photographic memory, Winslow had already memorized the entire script. But I didn't quite have my part down.

"Good afternoon, sir," I started, trying to project my voice enough to fill the room. "I seem to have gotten lost somehow. Can you direct me to Greece?"

"'I'm sorry,'" Winslow said quietly. "I am lost also. I have been trying to find Rome for some time now."

"Winslow, you can't just say it like you're reading it from a sheet of paper," I protested.

"You have to act it out."

"I don't know how to act." Winslow pushed his glasses up farther on his nose.

I sighed. It was definitely going to be a long afternoon.

Chapter Ten

When I woke up Monday morning, I jumped right out of bed and ran to the shower, thinking about all the things I had to do. It was going to be the busiest Monday of my entire life. While Sam was in the bathroom, I raced downstairs to the kitchen and put the invitation into his English book, which was in his knapsack by the back door. Knowing Sam, I was pretty sure that he wouldn't open the book until he got to class. Then I sat down to eat a bowl of cereal, propping my script up against the milk carton and reading it between bites.

I was really nervous about the skit, but I was looking forward to it, too. I've been in the school play every year since kindergarten, so I'm used to acting in front of a real audience. But this was different. This was for Mr. Grey. Even though I now knew he wasn't my secret admirer, I still wanted him to like the skit.

All through the day I kept looking over the script, making sure that I had absolutely, positively memorized every line. I didn't want anything to go wrong. Mr. Grey had told us that our special guests were members of the Board of Education, but what if one of them was actually a talent scout in disguise? Then maybe I would be discovered and get a part in a Broadway show! As soon as I thought of that, I started getting even more nervous.

The morning went by pretty quickly, and it was time for assembly before I knew it. When our turn came, I ran backstage to change. I was so nervous that I couldn't even put on my toga! First I put my head through the armhole, so I had all of this material hanging off the side. Then I put it on backward and the long piece that's supposed to sort of drape across the front got tangled around my neck. And poor Winslow was waiting in front of the whole audience by himself in a toga, with nothing to say!

Finally I got my toga on straight. But as I walked across the stage, my foot got caught in the hem. I had to get it loose before anyone noticed. I kicked my foot out in front of me. The bottom of my toga flew up in the air, and all of a sudden I realized that I'd forgotten to put on my sandals! I was still wearing my sneakers and socks! So much for authenticity. People were starting to laugh, and I could feel my body blush beginning.

I stared out toward the auditorium seats. Probably every single seventh grader at Bradley was looking at the stage and whispering that I had a crush on Winslow. The bright stage lights were on, so I couldn't see the audience very well, but I just knew that Mr. Grey and his guests were sitting there in the front row, probably taking notes. And they were all watching me and waiting for me to do something.

I told myself that I would be okay if I could just get into the skit, so I took a deep breath and got ready to say my first line. I opened my mouth and nothing came out. I couldn't remember my opening line! Winslow just stood there, staring at me. His eyes were getting wider and wider, and his ears were turning pink. *Winslow, give me a hint or something*, I thought, hoping he would read my mind. But he just kept standing there, staring.

My dreams of becoming an actress were flying out the window. I felt like I was going to die. My lips were dry and my mind was blank. Trying to remember, I looked out into the audience again. Then I heard Stacy Hansen start to laugh. It made me really angry. *How dare she laugh at me*, I thought. *I'll show her.* I took another deep breath, straightened my shoulders, and opened my mouth again.

"Good afternoon, sir. I seem to have gotten lost somehow," I said. "Can you direct me to Greece?"

It was my opening line! Winslow gave me a big, relieved smile and said his own line. After that I was fine. At the end we got more applause than any other group. Mr. Grey was really pleased. Even though things hadn't worked out for us, I still thought he was gorgeous. But thinking about that just reminded me of the mess I'd made out of the past week. And that reminded me of Sam. Now that the skit was over, I could concentrate on teaching him a lesson.

I went straight home from school after eighth period instead of going to Fitzie's with the girls. I wanted to find out if Sam had found the invitation. I sat down at the kitchen table, facing the back door, so that I could see him the second he walked in. I didn't have to wait long. I could hear someone whistling as he walked up the back steps.

The door slammed open and Sam stepped inside. He threw his knapsack on the floor, as he usually does, and tossed his coat on top of it. He was still whistling. He turned around, saw me, and gave me this huge smile. I knew right then that he'd found the invitation.

"Hey, Sabs! You did a great job on that skit today," he complimented me. He came over and patted me on the head, then walked over to the refrigerator. Sam was walking his "cool" walk, which he copied from our older brothers. He kind of swaggered with his hips moving back and forth. I tried not to giggle. Sam grabbed a Coke, walked back to the table, and sat down next to me. He was whistling again.

"How come you're so happy?" I asked, trying to act as innocent as possible.

"Me?" Sam said. "I'm always happy."

I took a quick sip of my own soda to keep from laughing at him. Always happy, huh? He might be happy now, but he'd definitely be whistling a different tune on Friday night. I smiled to myself at the thought.

Chapter Eleven

The week went by quickly. At five o'clock on Friday night, Katie, Allison, Randy, and I were gathered in the living room of my house. We wanted to see Sam's face when he came back from Stacy's, so I had asked my parents if the girls could come over to watch a movie on our VCR. After I'd promised that we weren't going to have another séance, they had said it was okay.

The four of us were sprawled on the floor in front of the television, munching on popcorn. Randy had brought a movie with her that she said we just had to see. It was called *Splatter University*. It was a horror film, of course, and we kept screaming every five minutes. Between screams I kept an eye on the front stairway.

At twenty minutes before six, Sam walked down the stairs. I nudged Katie, and she nudged Randy and Allison. He was wearing a dark-blue wool sweater with a white button-down shirt underneath. He had on his newest jeans, and there was a crease running all the way up the front. I knew that he had asked Mom to iron them for him. He was wearing his black high-top sneakers, which he only wears for special occasions, and his favorite pair of sunglasses.

"Phew!" said Randy, holding her nose. "What is that smell? I feel like I'm choking."

I sniffed the air. "P.U.!" I exclaimed. "Sam! How much cologne did you put on?"

Katie was holding a throw pillow to her nose, and even Allison was inching a little farther away.

"You have no taste," Sam told me, pulling out a comb and running it through his hair.

"I wish I had no sense of smell," Randy muttered under her breath.

Sam threw a dirty look in our direction, then walked down the hall and out the front door. The four of us started rolling around on the floor, laughing.

"I wish I could see his face," Katie gasped, holding her stomach.

"Yeah! It would be totally awesome to hide in the bushes and watch him ring the doorbell!" Randy said coolly.

"Randy!" I burst out. I stopped laughing and sat up. "That's a great idea! Let's hide in the bushes by Stacy's house and watch! If we hurry, we can get there just in time."

"I don't know..." Allison said, looking worried.

"I'm definitely going," Randy announced, jumping to her feet.

"Me too," Katie said. "This is so exciting!" She and Randy ran to get our coats from the kitchen.

"Allison? Are you coming?" I asked.

"You're sure we won't get in trouble?" she asked.

I nodded.

"Okay, then, let's go," Al said.

"Great!" I jumped up, pulled Al to her feet, and gave her a quick hug. "We'd better hurry."

I told my mom we were going for a walk. Then the four of us pulled on our coats and ran out the front door toward Stacy Hansen's house. We were only a block from her house when Katie, who was leading the way, suddenly stopped and ducked back around the corner. She motioned for us to stop, too.

"What's wrong?" I panted when I caught up with her.

"It's Sam," Katie told me. "He's right in front of us!"

I poked my head around the hedges on the corner. There he was, walking his cool walk and wearing his sunglasses.

"I feel like a spy," I said.

"Did he see you?" whispered Allison nervously.

"No," I assured her. "He's too busy daydreaming about Stacy. Anyway, I don't think he can see too well with those sunglasses on."

Now Randy was looking around the hedges. "I think it's safe for us to move now," she announced. "He just walked across the street."

"Where are we going to hide?" Allison asked. Her voice was shaking.

"The Hansens' next-door neighbors have bushes all along the property line," Randy told her. "We can crawl under them."

"Has he gone up to her house yet?"

Katie, who had been watching Sam from behind the mailbox on the corner, nodded. "He just walked up her front walk. Come on."

Quietly, keeping low to the ground, the four of us crept toward the house right next to Stacy's. We crawled along the ground under the bushes.

"Let's stop here," I whispered. "We'll have a perfect view of the front porch."

"This is incredible," Randy said. "It's like being the monster in a horror movie, watching the victim walk into a trap."

Sam was standing on the top step of Stacy's porch, with his hand reaching out to ring the doorbell. Even from fifty feet away, I could tell that his hand was shaking. I kept waiting for him to ring the bell, but he just stood there.

"Why isn't he ringing the doorbell?" Katie asked.

"He's trying to let that cologne air out some more," Randy muttered.

I had to bury my head in my arms to keep from laughing out loud. I could tell that Katie and Randy were doing the same thing. Allison just looked nervous.

Finally Sam rang the doorbell. He stepped back from the door, cleared his throat, and checked to make sure his collar was straight. He pulled his sunglasses off, then put them back on again. I was pretty sure he was blushing.

The door opened.

"Welcome to the...Sam? Sam Wells?" It was Stacy.

"Um...hi, Stacy," Sam squeaked.

I slapped my hands over my mouth to keep from laughing.

"What are *you* doing here?" Stacy demanded.

"I...we...you invited me," Sam said, sounding confused. "For dinner."

"I invited you for dinner?" said Stacy, her eyes wide. "Is this your idea of a joke?"

"No! I have the invitation right here." He dug into his pocket for the invitation. I held my breath.

"I don't have any idea what you're talking about, and I think you'd better..."

"Hey, Stacy! Who's at the door?" It was Laurel Spencer. Stacy already had someone at her house.

"This is even better than we planned," I whispered to the girls. They all nodded and went right back to listening.

"It's just Sam Wells," Stacy said, turning around." He says I invited him over for dinner." Even from behind the bushes I could see

Sam cringe.

"Dinner? Tonight?" Eva Malone came to the door, too. "That's crazy!"

"Did you say Sam Wells? Why is he here?" B.Z. Latimer pushed her way to the front steps. Something was funny about the way she looked. I inched forward to get a better look. Then I figured it out.

"Don't let him in here!" a couple of girls called from inside the house.

"But you invited me over for dinner," Sam protested, looking at Stacy.

Every girl on the porch started laughing hysterically.

"Hey, girls! Sam Wells says that Stacy invited him over for dinner tonight!" Eva called inside. All of a sudden there were about ten girls standing by the Hansens' front door in their nightgowns, laughing at Sam!

"Look, Sam," Stacy said, "I don't know what you're trying to do, but you can just forget about it. We're having a slumber party. And you weren't invited." Stacy motioned to all the girls on the porch. "Come on, let's go back inside."

When the girls had gone into the house, Stacy took one more look at Sam, started laughing all over again, and slammed the door in his face.

I looked at Katie, Randy, and Allison. They all had big smiles on their faces, and so did I. Mission accomplished! Sam was still standing on the porch, staring at the closed door, with his mouth hanging open. Then he looked down at the pale yellow invitation in his hand. With two quick rips he shredded it and threw it down on the front porch. Then he trudged down the steps and started walking back toward the street.

"Come on! We'll beat him back to the house!" I quickly scrambled out from under the bushes, with Randy, Katie, and Allison right behind me. The four of us waited until Sam had turned the corner, then we ran all the way around the block to get ahead of him. He was walking really slowly, so I knew it would take him forever to get home.

We ran all the way back to my house, dumped our jackets in the kitchen again, and brushed off all the dirt we'd collected from the bushes. Then we arranged ourselves in front of the television so that Sam wouldn't even know we had ever left. I had the newspaper on my lap.

When Sam walked in the front door about half an hour later, he looked like a completely different person. His hair was all tangled, his shirttail was hanging out, his shoelaces were untied, and his sunglasses were jammed into his pocket.

He came into the living room and sat on the arm of the couch, a dazed look on his face. Katie and Randy had their heads buried in two pillows, and their shoulders were shaking. Allison was biting her lip hard. It was taking every bit of acting talent I had to keep the serious expression on my face.

"Hi, Sam," I said sweetly. "Did you have a nice evening?"

"No," he said. "This is the worst night of my entire life."

Now Allison had to pick up a pillow to hold over her face. Randy and Katie were shaking so hard that I was afraid they were going to explode.

"Gee," I said, trying to keep the laughter out of my voice. "That's too bad." Sam looked at me closely, then at Randy, Al, and Katie. He stood up and walked over to me.

"Sabrina Wells," he began angrily, "you did this to me, didn't you? You set me up!"

I tried to look innocent.

"You put that note in my English book so I

would think Stacy Hansen put it there! Do you have any idea how stupid you made me feel? I can't believe you did this to me!"

"What's the matter, Sam?" I asked sweetly. *"Can't you take a joke?"*

Sam's face suddenly turned bright red. "You figured it out, didn't you? About the notes and the flowers and stuff?"

"Right," I said. "And now you know how it made me feel. I felt dumb, and embarrassed, and hurt. Probably the same way you're feeling now."

Sam just shook his head, and started to walk out of the room. "Hey, Sam!" I called after him. "What do you say we call it even! Just remember, don't believe everything you read."

Sam's face turned an even brighter shade of red, and he mumbled, "Okay, even." Then he ran up the stairs.

"Hey, Sabs," Katie asked when Sam left the room. "What *does* your horoscope say today?"

I opened the paper and read: *"A new friendship blossoms into love."*

Katie, Randy, and Allison looked at each other and screamed, "Winslow!"

Don't Miss
GIRL TALK #6
THE GHOST OF EAGLE MOUNTAIN

"I found us! I found us!" Katie called from the front of the crowd around the seventh-grade bulletin board.

"Where?" Sabrina asked quickly, standing on her toes to look over the shoulders of the people in front of her. "I can't see."

"It's the fifth column from the left," I told her, pointing it out. My name's Allison Cloud. I was standing with my best friends Sabrina, Randy, and Katie, and almost every other seventh grader at Bradley Junior High trying to read a list of names on the class bulletin board, trying to find their names.

"They put us all in the same cabin!" Katie announced.

"All right!" Sabrina said. "Three days on a snow-covered mountain . . ."

"They put the four of us together, all right," Randy grumbled. "Together with Stacy the Great and her clones!"

LOOK FOR THESE OTHER AWESOME
GIRL TALK BOOKS!

MORE GIRL TALK TITLES TO LOOK FOR

Nonfiction
ASK ALLIE 101 answers to your questions about boys, friends, family, and school!

YOUR PERSONALITY QUIZ Fun, easy quizzes to help you discover the real you!

BOYTALK: HOW TO TALK TO YOUR FAVORITE GUY